MONEY IS LIFE

Sucess if the key

DICKSON BLESSING

Dickson Blessing

I dedicate this book to every hard working man and women who are out there fighting for a better life. I want to thank you for all of your hard work, dedication, and sacrifice. You are the reason this book exists.

Thank you to my family who have always been there for me no matter what and have supported me through thick and thin. Thank you to my friends who have been there with me through thick and thin as well.

Thank you to my co-workers who laugh at my jokes, help me with my work, and make sure I don't go crazy at the end of the day.

And last but not least: Thank you to all of my readers out there who have been following along on this journey with me since day one! I hope that this book will help you in some way as well.

CONTENTS

INTRODUCTION

Hi! My name is Dickson Blessing and I'm a freelance writer. I specialize in writing articles for websites, blogs, and newsletters. I have experience writing news articles, product descriptions, and product reviews.

I've been writing since I was a kid, but never really thought of myself as a writer. It was just something that happened in my life—like breathing or blinking—and I didn't think about it much. But when I started college, one of my professors challenged me to write an article about something that interested me. That article led to another one, which led to many more—and now I spend my days writing for fun!

Writing is something that comes naturally to me. It's like breathing or blinking—something that happens without thinking about it at all! The best part is how much joy it brings me when someone else reads what I've written and enjoys it as much as I did while writing it!

MONEY IS LIFE.

You can't live life without it, and you definitely can't live the good life without it.

But it's hard to get money, isn't it? It's even harder to make money, and even harder to keep it.

That's why I wrote this book: because I want you to know how to make money, how to save money,
and how to use your money wisely so that you can use it for good.

The more money you have, the happier and more fulfilled you are.

If you want to get money and make sure your family is taken care of, here's what you need to do:

-Be patient. There will be ups and downs with money, but it's important that you stay consistent in your efforts.

-Be smart with your spending habits. You don't want to spend too much on things that don't really matter.
You don't want to spend too little, because then it's hard to get back up on track if something goes wrong or gets out of hand.

-Know when to say no before it becomes a problem for others or yourself! This is especially important at work—if
someone asks for something that isn't in line with company policy or if they're asking for something outside their job description,
let them know what needs to happen so the request doesn't turn into a problem later down the road.

I know you're thinking: "What do I need to do to get money?"

And the short answer is: not much!

Making money isn't a mystery. The real trick is doing the little things that really add up to make a big difference.
And the good news is that you don't need to work hard for your money. You just have to work smart!

There are so many ways to make money without even leaving your house. Even if you're a stay-at-home parent,
you can make a side income or have a full time income simply by working through tasks on the internet.
You can do this during your "free" time when your children are in school or whenever you want. If you want,
you can work evenings or weekends and still make money.

You just have to do what you're already doing. You have to be a good person, treat people with respect and kindness,
and put yourself in a position where people will want to help you.

The trick is not being lazy—it's just making sure you're working hard enough. And if you're willing to hustle for it,
then there are plenty of ways that you can make money without even leaving your house!

No matter who you are, everyone works the same way. Everyone wants the same things when they wake up in the morning.

Money. It's the root of all evil, and it's also the key to a better life.

If you're looking for a way to make more money, there are many ways to do that. But if you're not sure where to start,
here are some tips:

1 Look for ways to save money—you'll be amazed at how much you can save when you make little sacrifices on a regular basis.

2.Always try to do your best work, even if it means working harder than others think is necessary or possible.
That will only help you get ahead in the long run.

3.Learn as much as possible about your field, so that you can become an expert in what you do and know how
much value your skills bring to others' lives (and vice versa).

MONEY IS A BIG PART OF LIFE

Money is a big part of life—it's the fuel that drives our ability to live,
learn, and grow. But money doesn't just bring us a better quality of life;
it also brings us happiness. And if you're not happy? Well, that's kind of a big deal!

So how do you get money?

How do you make money?
And how do you fight for a better life?

You can start by asking yourself: What do I want from my life? What are my goals?

What are my values?

Then think about what skills and talents you have that could help you reach those goals.
Do they align with what you want in your life?
If they don't match up,
then maybe it's time to rethink what your goals are before looking at other ways to earn income.

But remember: no matter what kind of business venture or career path you choose,
there will be sacrifices made along the way.

Be sure those sacrifices are worth it—and remember that if

something doesn't seem like it's going right now,
there are always other options available to help turn things around!

WE'RE ALL ABOUT MONEY

If you're like most people, you're probably sick of hearing about the importance of money

It's the one thing that can't be taken away from us. And when we don't have enough of it, we feel like our lives are over

You've heard it in commercials, you've heard it from your parents and grandparents,
and you've probably even heard it from your co-workers. And while I'm not going to take away the importance of money—it's an essential part of life!—I do want to talk about how we can all make more of it.

But there is another way to get rich: you just need to know how to make money!
And it's not as hard as you think. In fact, there are so many ways to make money that it might just blow your mind!
Here's how you can start making a living without even having a job:

1) Start saving money in your piggy bank. You can do this by putting a small amount every day in an envelope and hiding it somewhere safe (like under your bed).
It doesn't matter where—just make sure nobody finds out about it!

2) When you've saved up enough money, sell something on Craigslist or eBay and make some extra cash! If you want more tips on how to sell things online,
check out our website or follow us on Twitter for all the info you need about selling stuff online for profit!

3)Make things with your hands (like furniture). If you don't know how to make furniture,
just Google "how to build a table" and find instructions online.

4)Sell online courses on Udemy (or any other site with an online course platform). Offer classes on topics like cooking,
fashion design, photography... anything that interests you!

5)Take freelance gigs as they come up. You may be able to get paid $10/hour at first but over time this can add up fast

6)Start a side hustle. You can sell your skills or offer services on TaskRabbit or TaskPoint (or any number of other sites).
Or if you're more creative than that, try making art or selling stuff on eBay for fun!

YOU WANT TO MAKE MONEY.

You want to make money. You want to get rich. You know that you can do it, but you're not sure how.

We've got some tips for you!

1. Get a job

It's really hard to make money when you don't have a job. Even if you're good at something else,
like building websites, or selling your art online, or making videos about how to wear shapewear,
the first thing people ask is "How much does that pay?" And if you don't have an answer?
Who will hire you? It's not just about getting paid;

it's about being able to live on what you earn and getting out of debt so that when you do get paid,
there's enough money left over for other things—like saving up for your dream vacation or buying yourself
a really nice dinner out tonight because you deserve it after working so hard at your job this week despite
having zero social life because everyone judges people based on what they do for work instead of who they are

2. Start investing early & invest wisely

Make Your Money Work for You,You probably have a 401(k) at your job, which is good.
But how many of your friends and family actually invest? Be the first to invest in yourself!
Investing early is the key to getting rich, but not all investments are as wise as others.

MONEY IS A KEY FACTOR IN EVERY MAN'S LIFE

Money is a key factor in every man's life. It can make or break you, and it's something that you have to constantly be aware of.

Money is an important aspect in every man's life. It's a powerful tool that can be used for good or for bad. Money can be used to buy things, but it also has the ability to change the way you see yourself and your world around you.

Every man should learn how to properly handle their finances, so they can use money as a tool to help them reach their goals, rather than being controlled by it.

The golden rules of money are as follows:

1. Never spend more than you earn

2. Save as much as possible

3. Invest in a diversified portfolio of investments

4. Never keep all your eggs in one basket

Money is important in every man's life, but it's especially important for men of color. And that's not just a matter of perception—it's a matter of fact.

We've been taught that money is power, and that without it we're useless. But this isn't true. In fact, it's the exact opposite:

without money, we're powerless.

Money is what allows us to access things like education and health care. It allows us to live in safe neighborhoods and buy the things we need to survive—like food and shelter—and enjoy the luxuries that make life more enjoyable.
Money gives us the ability to have better lives for ourselves and our families.

That's why it's so important for men of color to have as much money as possible: because when you don't have money, you can't do anything with your life or make other people's lives better.

MONEY IS A POWERFUL TOOL

Money is a powerful tool. It allows you to accomplish things that you may not have been able to otherwise.
It can make life easier, it can make your life more comfortable and it can help you live the life that you want.

The best thing about having money is that we are able to do things for other people, like our friends or family members.
We can buy them gifts, pay for their medical bills or even hire them on as a housekeeper or babysitter!

Now, imagine if you didn't have any money at all? How would your life change?
Would you still be able to buy things for your friends and family members? If so,
then maybe this article wasn't written for you after all! If not then read on...

Having money means that there are many things that we can do with it - from buying ourselves new clothes and shoes
every year (or every few years) to purchasing expensive cars or even going on holidays abroad;
we always seem to find something we want with our money!

Money is important because without it we wouldn't be able to do anything meaningful in this world - which

You might not think giving money to someone else is anything special—but it's actually pretty amazing!
You get to make their world better by giving them something they need, and they get something they want:
the gift of kindness from someone who cares about them.

Money is a powerful thing.

The kind of money that can get you out of a jam, or make your dreams come true. The kind of money
that can help you change your world, or give someone else a new lease on life.

It's not just what money can buy: it's also what money can do for you—and the person who has it.

Money can help you feel comfortable in your own skin and make choices based on your values and
needs rather than what's trendy or cool or expected.

Money can give others the opportunity to pursue their dreams and let go of their inhibitions,
so they can start living their lives fully.

People who have money often feel more satisfied with their lives and less stressed about making
ends meet because they know they'll always be able to take care of their families if something
happens (like losing a job).

People who don't have much money often don't feel as secure about their future,
because they're worried about how they'll pay for food, housing, health care—or even saving for retirement!

1. Money can buy you happiness

2. Money can make you feel good about yourself

3. Money can help you do the things you love to do etc.

SUCCESS IS THE KEY TO EVERYTHING

If you want to be successful, money is the key.

Money is life. Money is happiness. Money is what drives us all. Money makes the world go round.

But how do we get money? We don't just wake up one day and say "I'm going to make myself rich!"
or "I'm going to get rich!" It's not that easy—but it can be! If you want to be successful,
you've got to work for it and you've got to work hard for it, but once you do, there's nothing like it in this world.

If you want to be rich and successful in life, you need to realize that success is not an
end goal—it's a means to get where you want to go.
And once that's done, there are so many more things you can do with the money you've earned!

Money is power. Money is happiness. Money is freedom.

You can have all three, or you can have none of them!

When you're at the top of your game, it's easy to forget what makes you happy.

It's easy to feel like you're living a life without purpose or meaning.

But when you look back on your life, what do you see?

Do you see people who have succeeded in a way that makes them truly happy?

Do you see people who are truly successful?

The world needs more people like that.

When you are successful, people talk about you and they want to be around you.
You can get to where you want to go in life by being a leader and making sure that
everyone knows that you are the best at what you do. This means that every day,
it's important for you to work hard and make sure that everything is running smoothly so that no one feels
like they have to go above and beyond their job description.

That's the old saying, and it's true. When you're successful, people talk about you and they want to be around you.
It's hard to find someone who doesn't want to help you out when you're doing well.

But even if money isn't everything, it can make all the difference in how much fun your life is going to be.
Here are some ways to make sure that you're getting the most out of your money:

There are three things that are sure to make you successful:

1. You have to have a good head on your shoulders. You don't want to constantly be making bad decisions and letting yourself down.

2. You have to be willing to work hard for what you want in life

and that means putting in the time and effort it takes to achieve your goals.

3. You need to surround yourself with people who will support your dreams and help you achieve those goals,
because when you are successful people talk about you and they want to be around you!

But what if I told you that money doesn't make you happy? What if I told you that having more money doesn't actually make you happier?
What if I told you that if your goal in life is to get rich, then your life isn't going to be all that it could be?

What if I told you there are other ways of living a full and satisfying life?

Well, guess what—I am telling you! There are ways of living a life that doesn't revolve around money or status,
but instead focuses on the things that truly matter. If this sounds like something for which you'd be interested in exploring further, then keep reading!

I was once like you. I wanted to be rich and famous so badly that I did everything in my power to gain it all by any means necessary.
It didn't matter how unethical or immoral it was—if it meant getting what I wanted then it was fine with me.

But then something happened: I found out who I really was and what mattered most to me in life. And now, here's what has changed for me:

I no longer care about having money or power because those things aren't going to make me happy anymore. Instead, what matters most to me
is living a life of purpose and meaning—a life where every day is an opportunity for growth instead of a drag on my soul.

You're the CEO of your own company, or the manager at a company that has grown into a global success. You can make millions and millions of dollars,
and people will line up to hear what you have to say.

It's not just that they like what you have to say—but they want to be around it. They want to be near it, even if they don't know what it is yet.
They just know that it's something special, and they want a piece of it.

And when they have gotten their piece of that specialness, they keep coming back for more because their lives are better because they have been touched by it.
They know this might sound weird, but there are so many people out there who say things like "I was at your event last night" or "I saw this photo on Instagram"
or "your book really helped me through my [insert problem here]."

You see how this works?

IS MONEY EVERYTHING IN OUR LIFE

Is money everything in our life

No, money is not everything in our lives.

Of course, you can't be happy if you don't have enough money to buy things to make your life better, but happiness is not just about material things.
It's about other things too—like the love of family and friends and the joy of being able to do what you love every day.
It's also about having a sense of purpose that goes beyond making money and buying stuff.

Money isn't everything, but it's a good way to make sure that life is good!

Money is a powerful thing. It can help you achieve your goals, make life easier, and buy you things you really want. But money can also be a source of stress and anxiety.

Money is important to many people, but it's not everything. You can be happy without money, and that's okay! You don't have to feel like you're missing out on anything
if you don't have enough money—you just have to find other ways to get what matters most.

When you're young and in love, money seems like everything. You want to go on crazy adventures with your partner, buy them the best gifts,
travel the world... all of that takes money. But when you get older and have kids, your priorities change.
You want them to be healthy and safe—and that's not something you can do with a credit card.

And then there are things like paying for college and retirement, which should be covered by your employer or the government, but aren't always.

ABOUT THE AUTHOR

Dickson Blessing

Dickson Blessing is an award-winning author, editor, and speaker. He has written books on a variety of topics including business and spirituality.

Dickson Blessing is a social media manager . He's been working with content management and editorial strategy for over 10 years, and has been writing professionally since 2010.

PRAISE FOR AUTHOR

I'm so glad to have found this book. I've been looking for a book like this for years, and I think it's going to be really helpful for me.

ACKNOWLEDGEMENT

I'd like to start by thanking the following people, who have been instrumental in helping me get where I am today:

,Brian Tracy my mentor and friend who helped me get into this industry.

- My parents for introducing me to what it means to be a human and for their continued support.

- All of my co-workers who are always willing to lend an ear when I need help or advice.

- My friends, who are always there for me when times are tough.

www.ingramcontent.com/pod-product-compliance
Lightning Source LLC
LaVergne TN
LVHW020528160826
845677LV00015B/3956
9798847688758